The Tutter Family Reunion

Based on the TV series *Bear in the Big Blue House*™
created by Mitchell Kriegman. Produced by
The Jim Henson Company for Disney Channel.

 SIMON SPOTLIGHT
An imprint of Simon & Schuster Children's Publishing Division
1230 Avenue of the Americas
New York, New York 10020
Manufactured in the United States of America
First Edition   10 9 8 7 6 5 4 3 2 1
ISBN 0-689-84022-5

The Tutter Family Reunion

by Nancy Inteli
based on a teleplay by P. Kevin Strader
illustrated by Tom Brannon

Simon Spotlight

New York   London   Toronto   Sydney   Singapore

It was a busy day at the Big Blue House. Tutter was hosting the annual Tutter Family Reunion. Grandma Flutter came over early to help.

"Thank you for letting us use your house, Bear," said Grandma Flutter as she sliced some cheddar cheese.

"Oh, Bear," said Tutter nervously. "We're never going to be ready!"

"Sure we will," Bear answered calmly. "I'm going to see how things are coming along."

Bear found Pip and Pop hard at work cleaning the living room.

"Don't worry about those cobwebs on the ceiling, Pop," said Bear. "I don't think Tutter's family can see all the way up there."

"But what if they bring in a trampoline and start jumping really high?" asked Pop.

"Hmm, good point," Bear said with a chuckle. "Keep up the good work!"

Outside, Treelo and Ojo were hanging balloons and a welcome sign.

"I can't wait to meet Tutter's Uncle Tito del Tutter," Ojo said to Treelo. "He's a great flamenco dancer."

"Treelo like dancing," Treelo said.

Bear watched as Ojo and Treelo decorated the porch. He was looking forward to meeting Tutter's relatives, too.

Bear went back into the kitchen. "Pip, Pop, Ojo, and Treelo are doing a great . . . ," he started to say. But no one was there. "Uh, Tutter? Grandma Flutter?"

"Oh, great Gouda!" Bear heard Tutter say. "It has to be here somewhere, Grandma."

"What's wrong, Tutter?" Bear asked.

"We made everything except the Tutter Family Loaf," said Tutter.

"We always save that for last," Grandma Flutter added.

"It's a special recipe that has thirteen kinds of cheese," Tutter explained. "But we don't have any Swiss cheese. We can't make the Tutter Family Loaf with only twelve kinds of cheese!"

"I think I can help," Bear said. "Doc Hogg just brought over a gift basket full of Swiss cheese."

"Thank you, Bear. Thank you so much!" Tutter exclaimed, "It wouldn't have been a Tutter Family Reunion without the cheese loaf."

"And it wouldn't be a Tutter Family Loaf without Swiss cheese," added Grandma Flutter.

Soon the food was ready, the house was cleaned, and the balloons and banner were hung.

"It looks like we're ready for our guests," said Ojo.

"No, not yet," Tutter said. "There's still work to be done in my mouse hole! I have to bring out all my photo albums."

"Ooh, can we see them?" asked Pip and Pop together.

Tutter went into his mouse hole. When he came back out, his arms were filled with photo albums.

"There's always time to look at pictures," Tutter said.

"This is Tardy," said Tutter.
"Why is he all alone?" asked Pip.
"Tardy Tutter is always late," Grandma Flutter said.
"For that party, he arrived so late that everyone else was gone!" Tutter explained.

"Look, here's a picture of Grandpa Highland McTutter," said Grandma Flutter. "He plays the bagpipes at our reunion every year."

"Maybe he can teach us how to play bagpipes," said Pip. "That would be fun!" said Pop. As Pip and Pop imagined themselves playing bagpipes like Grandpa Highland McTutter, the doorbell rang.

"They're here!" Tutter gasped.

Tutter was excited to greet his first guest.
"*Hola,*" said Tito del Tutter when Bear opened the door.

Soon the Big Blue House was filled with little, blue Tutters. Everyone was having a great time.

Tutter couldn't have been happier—until he overheard Whiner Tutter complaining. "There is hardly any cheese in this cheesarita," he whined. "Yeah, this must not be the real family recipe!" Shouter Tutter shouted.

Bear found Tutter moping outside his mouse hole. "What's wrong, Tutter?" he asked. "Whiner and Shouter said bad things about the food," Tutter said.

"It's always hard to please a big group," said Bear. "Sometimes you just can't make everyone happy."

Just then, Tutter was called into his mouse hole.

"I have to go," Tutter said.

As soon as Tutter walked in, his family cheered.
"Hooray, Tutter!" everyone yelled.
Tutter was surprised. Not only did Tutter's family want him to slice the family cheese loaf, but they made a special speech in his honor!

At the end of the day, the Tutters started getting ready to head home.

"This sure was a great reunion," said Jim Tutter. "And your Tutter Family Loaf was delicious."

"Really?" asked Tutter.

"Most definitely," said June Tutter.

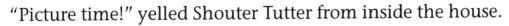

"Picture time!" yelled Shouter Tutter from inside the house.

"Please stay for the reunion photo," said Grandma Flutter.

"Of course! We wouldn't miss it for the all the cheddar in the world," said June.

Just then a little car pulled up in front of the Big Blue House and a mouse scurried out. "Am I late?" asked Tardy Tutter.

"Wow! Even Tardy is here," said a happy Tutter as everyone smiled for the camera. "Say cheese!" they shouted.